Fact Finders®

MEDIA LITERACY

COMING DISTRACTIONS

Questioning Movies

by Frank W. Baker

Capstone
press®

Mankato, Minnesota

Fact Finders is published by Capstone Press,
151 Good Counsel Drive, P.O. Box 669, Mankato, Minnesota 56002.
www.capstonepress.com

Library of Congress Cataloging-in-Publication Data
Baker, Frank W.
    Coming distractions : questioning movies / by Frank W. Baker.
    p. cm.—(Fact Finders. Media literacy)
    Summary: "Describes what media is, how movies are part of media, and encourages readers to
question the medium's influential messages"—Provided by publisher.
    Includes bibliographical references and index.
    ISBN-13: 978-0-7368-6766-5 (hardcover)
    ISBN-10: 0-7368-6766-X (hardcover)
    ISBN-13: 978-0-7368-7862-3 (softcover pbk.)
    ISBN-10: 0-7368-7862-9 (softcover pbk.)
    1. Motion pictures—Juvenile literature. I. Title. II. Series.
PN1994.5.B27 2007
791.43—dc22   2006021441

Editorial Credits

Jennifer Besel, editor; Juliette Peters, designer; Jo Miller, photo researcher/photo editor;
    Tami Collins, illustrator

Photo Credits

Capstone Press/Karon Dubke, 4 (*Lost* image, books), 7 (movie images), 8 (all), 9 (people), 13, 14 (all),
16 (DVD covers), 17, 18, 20, 21 (movie image), 23 (poster, hands, computer), 24 (all), 25 (CD covers),
26 (all), 29 (all); Capstone Press/TJ Thoraldson Digital Photography, 4 (magazine); Comstock Images,
cover (box of popcorn); Corbis/Bureau L.A. Collection, 9 (camera); Corbis/John Springer Collection,
28 (*Great Train Robbery*); Corbis/Rick Doyle, 19; Courtesy of Frank W. Baker, 32; Getty Images Inc./Paul
Hawthorne, 12; Getty Images Inc./Photographer's Choice/Joe McBride, 11 (child); Getty Images Inc./
Warner Brothers, 28 (*The Jazz Singer*); Shutterstock/Duasbaew Alisher, 4 (TV); Shutterstock/Lancelot et
Naelle, cover (cinema room); Shutterstock/Lorelyn Medina, 7, 16, 21, 27 (popcorn images); The Kobal
Collection/NBC-TV, 23 (talk show); The Kobal Collection/Universal, 6; ZUMA Press/Copyright 2003
by Courtesy New Line Cinema, 25 (Gollum); ZUMA Press/Copyright 2005 by Courtesy of Columbia
Pictures/Jaimie Trueblood, 10; ZUMA Press/Universal Pictures, 15

The author would like to dedicate this book to Bryan and Josh, his movie-going buddies.

1 2 3 4 5 6 12 11 10 09 08 07

TABLE OF CONTENTS

I'll Take a "Medium," Please...................... 4

Roll the Credits................................ 6

Now Showing: *Marketing Mania* 10

Would You Like a Value with That? 14

The Magical World of Movies.................. 18

Creating the Buzz............................. 22

Time Line 28

Glossary 30

Internet Sites 31

Read More 31

Index 32

Meet the Author 32

Are you sitting down right now? Well, stand up and take a look around. I bet the room is full of **media**. It's the TV playing in the background. It's the magazine on your bed. This book is even part of the media. Media is everywhere! (Oh, you can sit down now.)

So, what is this "media," you ask? Media is how we get our information and our entertainment. It also tells us all kinds of things about the world around us. Media messages inform, entertain, or even persuade us. But media messages all have one thing in common—they **influence** us.

The media, especially movies, is fun. There's no doubt about that. But sometimes media doesn't give us the whole story. And that can be a problem. But never fear! There is an easy way to make sure we aren't influenced without knowing it. Think about what you see and ask questions.

QUESTION IT!

Who made the message and why?

Who is the message for?

How might others view the message differently?

What is left out of the message?

How does the message get and keep my attention?

ROLL THE CREDITS

Who made the message and why?

All moviemakers create films for a purpose. For most, the purpose is to make money. Movie studios are always trying to make the next blockbuster film.

But selling tickets isn't the only way movies make money. Some companies pay to put their products in films. The idea here is that seeing a famous person using the product will make you want to use it too. It's called product placement. Next time you watch a movie, watch for name brand products to pop up. And know they aren't there by accident.

LINGO

blockbuster: a movie that makes more than $100 million dollars

product placement: putting products and logos in movies so moviegoers will see them

Can you find the product placement? Hint: Look at Adam Sandler's shirt or the caddy's hat!

REALITY CHECK

Some movies have products placed everywhere. The 2002 movie *Spider-Man* is one of them. More than 20 products were carefully placed throughout the film. Company logos like Prudential and Cingular are displayed on billboards in the background. Other products are featured more heavily. Who knew Spider-Man wore Nike shoes? Dr. Pepper and Tropicana orange juice must be the superhero's favorite beverages. Look closely the next time you pop *Spider-Man* into the DVD player. See what other products you can spot.

It takes hundreds of people to make a movie. Everyone has their own role and responsibility. But they all have to work together to create a film.

The **SCRIPTWRITER** writes the screenplay, telling what will happen in the movie and what the characters will say.

The person managing the film process and the costs is the **PRODUCER**.

The **DIRECTOR** is in charge of actually making the film.

Not all films are shot in a studio. The **SCOUT**'s job is to find locations to shoot the film.

Without the **CINEMATOGRAPHER** there wouldn't be a movie. Her job is to film the action with a camera.

The **ACTORS** get the most fame. They are the characters we see on the big screen when the movie is finished.

Who is the message for?

I bet you didn't know that we are important parts of the movie-making process. We help filmmakers decide what movies to make and how to **market** them. (So, where's my paycheck?)

Filmmaking is all about making films that people pay to see. But moviemakers aren't dumb. They know that not everyone will be interested in every movie. Before a movie is filmed, they know exactly who their movie is for.

Filmmakers kept their target audience in mind as they shot this scene from *Lords of Dogtown*.

Just What You Wanted to See

Audience research helps movie studios know what their target audience likes and what they expect. Companies get this information from focus groups and questionnaires. They also study how the audience reacted to similar movies.

From the research, they know Grandma won't want to see *Revenge of the Mighty Hamburger*. But they think you just might be interested. Say they find out from their research that most kids your age really like skateboarding. Well, you can bet that the Mighty Hamburger will show up on a skateboard during an action-packed scene.

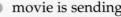

LINGO

target audience: the group of people that moviemakers think will be interested in the message the movie is sending

That's some sweet air! Don't be surprised to see something this cool end up in a movie like *Revenge of the Mighty Hamburger.*

Testing It Out

Once a film is almost finished, moviemakers show their film to a test audience. This group is made up of people that marketers think fit into the target audience. These people get to see the movie before it's released. In exchange, they rate the film, telling moviemakers what they liked or disliked.

Sometimes test audience reviews come back with not-so-good results. Filmmakers take negative comments seriously. In fact, bad reviews just might cause them to redo parts of the movie. Filmmakers and studios know that if the target audience doesn't like the film, the film won't sell.

LINGO

MGM: short for Metro-Goldwyn-Mayer Inc.; MGM is a movie studio that has made hundreds of movies such as *Rocky*, *All Dogs Go to Heaven*, and *Legally Blonde*.

TRY IT OUT!

Suppose MGM thinks women ages 60–75 are an audience that would spend money at the movies. They need you to come up with a movie idea. Grab a notebook and pencil. Write down some movie ideas you think your grandma would enjoy. Here are some questions to get you started.

- What do you think older women enjoy?
- What do older women dislike?
- What actors might attract this audience?

When you're done, pick the best idea. Ask someone in that target audience what they think of your idea. See if you knew what the audience wanted.

WOULD YOU LIKE A VALUE WITH THAT?

How might others view the message differently?

Ever wonder why your dad didn't find that *Mighty Hamburger* movie funny? Well, it's simple. Nobody has exactly the same values. Values are what you think is important or true. Age, gender, and life experiences all affect your values.

Age and life experiences generally go hand in hand. What was interesting when you were little might be boring now. Marketers know that values affect how we feel about a movie. They use this information to send their messages to just the right people.

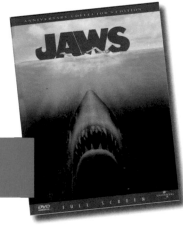

Shark Tale is fun for a younger audience, but the makers of *Jaws* had an older audience in mind.

Men and Women

Gender can also play a role in what we think about a movie. Marketers pay special attention to this fact. Women are often attracted to movies about relationships. So romantic comedies, also known as chick flicks, are directly marketed to women.

Moviemakers don't expect men to spend a lot of money to see romantic comedies. But the opposite can be true for action movies. These movies are targeted to men. Marketers use things like fast cars and beautiful women to catch the eyes of this target audience.

The action film *The Fast and the Furious* was a big hit with its target audience. Any guesses who that was?

15

REALITY CHECK

We all know that action movies, romantic comedies, and comedies make big bucks at the box office. But adults aren't the only ones watching movies. In 2005, six of the year's 19 blockbusters were marketed to kids. Coming in at number 2 for the year, *The Chronicles of Narnia: The Lion, the Witch, and the Wardrobe*, made just under $300 million. *Harry Potter and the Goblet of Fire* was right behind at number 3. *Charlie and the Chocolate Factory* made just over $200 million. *Madagascar*, *Chicken Little*, and *Robots* all made the top 15 **grossing** movies of 2005, making well over $100 million each.

Values at the Movies

Movies **promote** values by showing us how characters look, behave, and feel. Sometimes these values influence how we think about our world.

Stereotypes are part of the values a movie promotes. Most movie heroes are good-looking. But villains are often ugly. Does that mean pretty people are good while ugly people are bad?

Movie stereotypes creep up in other ways too. People of color are often the bad guys in films. But is that reality? Are people of color always criminals? No! But if movies influence how you see the world you might think so. That's why questioning movies is so important.

Some movies marketed to kids, like *Agent Cody Banks*, have stereotyped bad guys.

17

What is left out of the message?

Every time cinematographers look through their camera they frame their shot. They focus on one thing. But just as important as what's in their frame is what isn't. Sometimes moviemakers leave things out of the frame or out of the script on purpose. But why would they do that? Well, there are a few reasons.

The "Butt-numbing" Effect

One reason filmmakers leave things out is simply a length issue. If our butts fall asleep because the movie is too long, we're not going to like it. Moviemakers have to decide what to keep and what to cut.

The movie *Harry Potter and the Goblet of Fire* was more than two hours long. Can you imagine how long it would be if they put everything from the book into the film?

Painting a "Bad" Picture

Sometimes movies leave things out that would make them lose **momentum**. Fast-paced, action-packed car chase movies are exciting to watch. Violent fight scenes are thrilling to see. But movies don't always show the effects of these actions.

Watching people clean up the damage or go to the hospital just isn't as fun. So even though the movie is entertaining, we have to remember that it's not really how things would go down in real life.

LINGO

frame: to focus the camera on an object or scene

TRY IT OUT!

Imagine that you're writing a screenplay about your life. It's getting long, so you have to decide what to leave out. Make a list of the things you would not put in a movie about you. Here are some things to consider.

- Do you show your bad habits? Why or why not? If you don't, does that change the story of the real you?

- Do you include situations where you got in trouble? Why or why not?

Painting a "Pretty" Picture

Think about a movie dealing with ordinary people with real problems. Maybe a dad loses his job. Even without a job, the family still has a brand new car, a beautiful home, and fashionable clothes. How can they afford it? Moviemaking magic, that's how. A leading man doesn't look as good driving a rusty old car. A leading lady, even when she's fighting the bad guys, wears high heels. These tricks make for entertaining viewing, but they don't paint an accurate picture of real life.

Cameron Diaz in *Charlie's Angels* makes fighting in heels look easy.

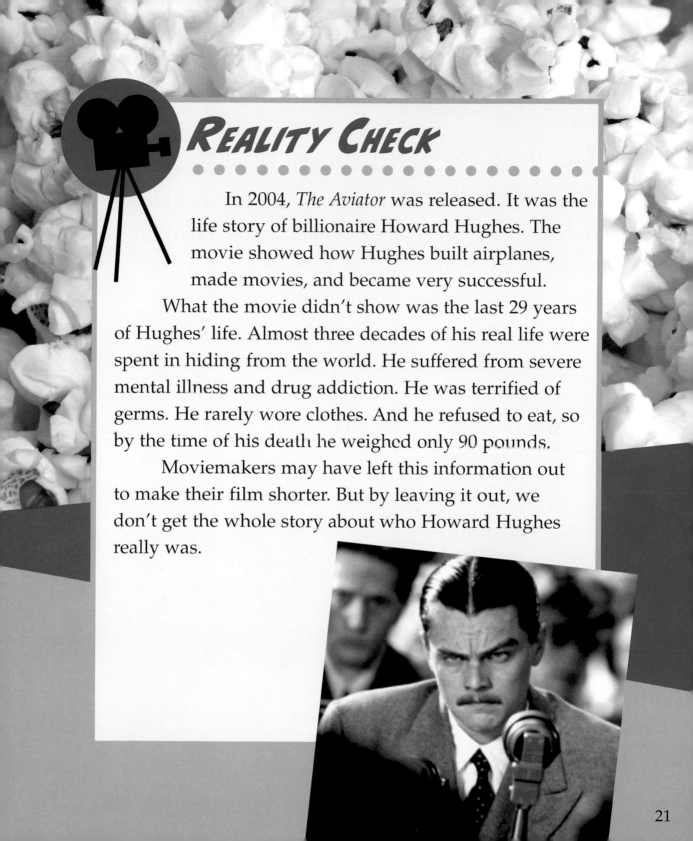

REALITY CHECK

In 2004, *The Aviator* was released. It was the life story of billionaire Howard Hughes. The movie showed how Hughes built airplanes, made movies, and became very successful.

What the movie didn't show was the last 29 years of Hughes' life. Almost three decades of his real life were spent in hiding from the world. He suffered from severe mental illness and drug addiction. He was terrified of germs. He rarely wore clothes. And he refused to eat, so by the time of his death he weighed only 90 pounds.

Moviemakers may have left this information out to make their film shorter. But by leaving it out, we don't get the whole story about who Howard Hughes really was.

CREATING THE BUZZ

How does the message get my attention?

So now we know studios think a lot about who the movie is for, what they'd put in the movie, and what to leave out. But how do they get the word out? Movie studios **advertise** their movies like crazy. They market their films in places where their target audience will see it. Trailers for *Revenge of the Mighty Hamburger* won't be running during the evening news. Kids aren't watching TV then. But they'll be all over the TV right around the time school lets out!

Movie studios use more than trailers to grab our attention. They use every marketing trick in the book.

Movie posters tell important features about a movie. They list the title, the stars, and what happens.

Stars of the movie give lots of interviews on TV, on the radio, in magazines, and even on Web sites. Moviemakers hope the more you hear about the movie, the more interested you'll be.

Blogs are becoming a popular way to promote movies. Bloggers write about movies to create more buzz.

Movie critics get to see movies before the public. Their reviews carry a lot of weight. Many people will go to see a movie that gets "two thumbs up."

23

How does the message keep my attention?
Mixing Up a Movie

It takes a lot of ingredients to mix up a film. These ingredients all have to work together to keep us in our seats. Why does that matter? Well, if we aren't interested, we won't buy the products featured in the film or tell our friends to buy tickets.

LIGHTS...

The position of the lights can tell us a lot about what's happening. A character in a well-lit area is safe and happy. When a person's face is half in shadow, half in light we know she is doing something evil.

LINGO

pan: to move the camera back and forth

CAMERA...

In a movie, we only see what the camera sees. And moviemakers use this to their advantage. In a scene in *Jaws*, the director wanted the shark's point of view. So the camera became the shark. When the "shark" moved, the camera was panned. We don't see the shark, but we know it's after the swimmer.

ACTION!

Moviemakers use CGI (Computer Generated Imagery) to keep the action going. Dangerous or imaginary scenes can be digitally created to look like anything they want. The character Gollum from the *Lord of the Rings* trilogy was made using CGI.

ADD THE MUSIC

Could you imagine *Star Wars* without the music? Music is a great trick to keep our attention. Generally, we don't even think about the music. But without it, movies just wouldn't be as exciting. Did you know editors dub in the sound track after the movie is filmed? The actors may not even hear the finished sound track until they see the final cut of the movie.

LINGO

dub: adding a sound track to a movie after filming is complete

Jolts Per Minute

Lighting, music, camera angles, and special effects are all ingredients that make movies exciting and fun. But moviemakers have other tricks they use to keep us watching. One of these tricks is called jolts per minute (JPM). JPMs are fast, exciting quick cuts or action sequences that get you excited. Need an example? Pop *Shrek* into the DVD player. Go to the part where Shrek, Donkey, and Princess Fiona are being chased by the dragon. During that sequence the scene changes every couple seconds. See how exciting and jolting those quick cuts are?

LINGO

quick cut: fast scene changes that are meant to jolt and excite you

The End

Movies are great entertainment. And sometimes they even teach us a thing or two. That's why we watch them. What's cool, though, is that we don't have to believe everything a movie shows. It's totally our choice. So let's go pop some popcorn, watch a movie, and enjoy asking questions.

TRY IT OUT!

Music can play a big role in a movie's JPMs. Suppose *Revenge of the Mighty Hamburger* needs a sound track. Get out your CD collection. Pick out some songs that would fit these scenes.

• The Mighty Hamburger is rolling down the hill on his skateboard going 60 miles per hour. The cops are chasing him and getting closer and closer.

• The Mighty Hamburger and a beautiful cheeseburger take a stroll along the beach at sunset.

Did you use different kinds of music for each scene? Why or why not? Could you use something other than music to beef up a movie's JPMs?

TIME LINE

The film *Workers Leaving the Factory in Lyon* is the first film shown in a public screening.

The Jazz Singer, the first feature-length movie with sound, is released.

Reese's Pieces are placed in *ET, the Extra Terrestrial*. It's the first use of branded product placement in a movie.

1895   1903   1923   1928   1982

The Great Train Robbery becomes the first American movie to tell a complete story.

The first animated movie with sound, Walt Disney's *Steamboat Willie*, is released.

Spider-Man is released. The film features more than 20 product placement ads.

Six of the year's 19 blockbuster movies are for kids, proving that kids are a profitable target audience.

1995   2002   2004   2005

First 100% computer animated movie, *Toy Story*, is released.

The Aviator is released. It's a film about Howard Hughes that leaves out almost 30 years of his life.

GLOSSARY

advertise (AD-ver-tize)—to give information about something you want to sell

gross (GROHSS)—to earn or bring in

influence (IN-floo-uhnss)—to have an effect on someone or something

market (MAR-kit)—to sell

media (MEE-dee-uh)—a group of mediums that communicates messages; one piece of the media, like movies, is called a medium.

momentum (moh-MEN-tuhm)—the speed or force something has when it's moving

promote (pruh-MOTE)—to make the public aware of something or someone

stereotype (STER-ee-oh-tipe)—an overly simple opinion of a person, group, or thing

INTERNET SITES

FactHound offers a safe, fun way to find Internet sites related to this book. All of the sites on FactHound have been researched by our staff.

Here's how:

1. Visit *www.facthound.com*

2. Choose your grade level.

3. Type in this book ID **073686766X** for age-appropriate sites. You may also browse subjects by clicking on letters, or by clicking on pictures and words.

4. Click on the **Fetch It** button.

FactHound will fetch the best sites for you!

READ MORE

Ali, Dominic. *Media Madness: An Insider's Guide to Media*. Tonawanda, N.Y.: Kids Can Press, 2005.

Jones, Sarah. *Film*. Media Wise. North Mankato, Minn: Smart Apple Media, 2003.

Pelusey, Michael, and Jane Pelusey. *Film and Television*. The Media. Philadelphia: Chelsea House, 2005.

INDEX

advertising, 22
attention-getting tricks, 22–23
attention-keeping tricks,
    24–25, 26, 27
audience research, 11

influence, 4, 5, 17

jolts per minute, 26, 27

marketers, 12, 14, 15
marketing, 10, 15, 16, 22
media, 4, 5
missing information, 5, 18, 19,
    20, 21, 22
movie studios, 6, 11, 13, 22, 23

product placements, 6, 7, 24

quick cuts, 26

stereotypes, 17

target audiences, 10, 11, 12, 13,
    14, 15, 16, 22
test audiences, 12, 13

values, 14, 17

who makes movies, 8–9
why movies are made, 6

MEET THE AUTHOR

Frank Baker is an educational consultant, bringing media literacy to the classroom. In addition to maintaining his nationally recognized Web site, The Media Literacy Clearinghouse (www.frankwbaker.com), Frank is a frequent presenter at schools and conferences across the United States.